READING CORNER

Sing-Song
Mum

A humorous story
in a familiar setting

First published in 2004 by
Franklin Watts
96 Leonard Street
London
EC2A 4XD

Franklin Watts Australia
45–51 Huntley Street
Alexandria
NSW 2015

A CIP catalogue record for this book is available
from the British Library.

ISBN 0 7496 5745 6 (hbk)
ISBN 0 7496 5783 9 (pbk)

Series Editor: Jackie Hamley
Series Advisors: Dr Barrie Wade, Dr Hilary Minns
Design: Peter Scoulding

Printed in Hong Kong / China

For Jago with love – A.A.

Sing-Song Mum

Written by
Joan Stimson

Illustrated by
Anni Axworthy

FRANKLIN WATTS
LONDON•SYDNEY

Joan Stimson

"I can't sing at all, but I can be very noisy when I get excited. I hope you enjoy the book!"

Anni Axworthy

"I liked drawing these pictures because I'm a sing-song mum, too. Luckily, my little boy likes to join in when I sing!"

Mike's mum liked to sing.

She sang in the bath.

She sang on the bus.

She sang in the park.

She sang at the pool.

When his mum sang,

Mike went pink.

And when she sang in front of his friends, Mike went red all over.

One day, Mike asked his friend
Dave to come and play.

15

"Please, Mum," said Mike,

"when Dave comes, don't sing!"

17

When Dave came, Dave's dad
walked over with him.

Mike and his mum heard Dave's
dad before they saw him.

"I'm sorry," said Dave.

"My dad likes to sing."

22

23

"And sometimes he sings *in front of my friends!*" said Dave.

25

Dave went pink ...

... then red.

But Mike didn't.

"Your dad and my mum can have a sing-song," said Mike.

"And we can play quietly
on my drum kit!"

Notes for parents and teachers

READING CORNER has been structured to provide maximum support for new readers. The stories may be used by adults for sharing with young children. Primarily, however, the stories are designed for newly independent readers, whether they are reading these books in bed at night, or in the reading corner at school or in the library.

Starting to read alone can be a daunting prospect. READING CORNER helps by providing visual support and repeating words and phrases, while making reading enjoyable. These books will develop confidence in the new reader, and encourage a love of reading that will last a lifetime!

If you are reading this book with a child, here are a few tips:

1. Make reading fun! Choose a time to read when you and the child are relaxed and have time to share the story.

2. Encourage children to reread the story, and to retell the story in their own words, using the illustrations to remind them what has happened.

3. Give praise! Remember that small mistakes need not always be corrected.

READING CORNER covers three grades of early reading ability, with three levels at each grade. Each level has a certain number of words per story, indicated by the number of bars on the spine of the book, to allow you to choose the right book for a young reader:

GRADE 1	GRADE 2	GRADE 3
50 words	130 words	250 words
70 words	160 words	350 words
100 words	200 words	450 words